A FINE POINT OF MURDER

A VALENTINE'S DAY COZY MYSTERY

THEA CAMBERT

SUMMER PRESCOTT BOOKS PUBLISHING

Copyright 2022 Summer Prescott Books

All Rights Reserved. No part of this publication nor any of the information herein may be quoted from, nor reproduced, in any form, including but not limited to: printing, scanning, photocopying, or any other printed, digital, or audio formats, without prior express written consent of the copyright holder.

**This book is a work of fiction. Any similarities to persons, living or dead, places of business, or situations past or present, is completely unintentional.

CHAPTER 1

When you drive across the Confederation Bridge, which stretches across the Abegweit Passage of the Northumberland Strait, there might be a moment when you wonder how long a bridge can be, and whether this one will actually take you anywhere. For nearly thirteen kilometers—over eight miles—you will be suspended above the water, and there is that moment when the mainland has disappeared, but the island is not yet in sight. That is the moment of faith that all islands require of those who wish to touch their shores, and you will feel it, whether by bridge or by ferry or by air. There is a leap of faith to be made.

The reward to the faithful, of course, is the island itself. That's what Olive Martin was thinking as she exited the bridge and her wheels touched ground on the island, *her* island. In spite of the February chill, she opened her window briefly as she made the eastward turn toward Charlottetown and breathed in the cold salt air. Some things, at least, never changed.

She'd grown up on Prince Edward Island—yes, that fabled home of Ann and her charming Green Gables—and her roots there were deeply woven down into the sandy red soil. Just shy of Charlottetown, the island's capitol, she veered north—the road as familiar to her as the back of her own hand. She had been too long on the mainland, and she hadn't even realized it until now. There had been university, then art school, then a steady job in New Brunswick (quite a feat for a bookbinder), then a steady boyfriend, then loss of said boyfriend, and now, somehow, she was thirty-two and had only been to her island here and there, now and then, over the past decade. She'd come to visit her dad and see old friends . . . coming and going again, always in a bit of a blur.

But now she was home and how long this trip would be, she had no idea. Her dad needed her, and she would stay until . . . until he didn't.

The town of St. Drogo was home to only a couple thousand souls. It lay among the gentle hills that roll to the north and south of the coasts, tucked between the strait and the Gulf of St. Lawrence, now blanketed in snow. Founded back in 1860, the town had long held tight to its Victorian heritage, evident in its architecture and cobblestone sidewalks. There had always been some debate as to how the town had gotten its name, as St. Drogo is patron saint of both coffeehouses and unattractive people. Legend had it that the founders were indeed lovers of a good cup of joe—but were also not particularly attractive—so it was really anyone's guess.

As Olive turned onto Forest Lane—one of the four main streets that wrapped themselves around the center of town, she felt a rush of memories. The great trees that arched and stretched across the street still stood guard over the bricked storefronts, including the quiet corner of Forest and Wellington Street where her father and his father and *his* father had lived and worked through the generations. Olive rolled to a stop in front of Martin and Son and smiled up at the beautiful old building. There was the shop downstairs and the lovely home above it on the second and third floors. Olive had grown up here, had run up and down those front steps a billion times, had earned spending money working in the shop after school.

The Martins were stationers. Paper, envelopes, pens . . . carefully curated items for people who were serious about their writing, for those discerning few who still valued the handwritten word, decent penmanship, fine paper. Olive dug through her bag and produced her key, then climbed the outside staircase that led up to the second floor—which could be reached from inside too, but that would require her to walk through the shop. She opened the door and paused. *Home.* She walked through the shafts of sunlight that washed the room, pouring in through huge windows. The large old apartment had always felt like more of a treehouse to Olive. She remembered looking out her bedroom window, watching birds build their nests in the accommodating branches just outside.

She looked out those very windows now and felt the warmth of the years of playing and daydreaming and dancing through this space. It felt safe. If only her dad was here, it would've been perfect. But that was why he needed her—because he was in the hospital.

About a week earlier, Henry Martin's assistant at Martin and Son, Malcolm Warbly, had suddenly fallen ill, had been admitted to St. Drogo Regional Hospital, and just a few days ago, had passed away to everyone's surprise. That was alarming enough. But then a few days ago, Henry had developed the same symptoms. Intestinal pain and upset, and as he'd been around Malcolm so much, there was a real chance he had caught the same illness. Olive put her things on her bed and called the hospital. She was told her father had finally fallen asleep, but that she could come visit in a bit, so she decided to go downstairs to check in at the shop before heading over to the hospital.

She took the stairs two at a time and emerged into the most wonderful place on earth: the stationery shop.

CHAPTER 2

Olive had been enchanted by paper goods for as long as she could remember. Notebooks, journals, stationery . . . just the smell of good paper made her feel comfortable in the same way that a child who grows up on the river will always feel at home when he smells the river smells.

Martin and Son sold more than just paper. They boasted an excellent selection of fine pens—mostly fountain, but some rollerball, gel, ballpoint, and brush as well. And of course, they had a thoughtfully curated collection of inks on offer, both in bottles and in cartridges. They offered custom stationery and invitations and announcements made to order. And then there were some carefully chosen crafting and art supplies, planners, notebooks, and reams of quality paper. There was even a small grouping of books—mostly reference books. You could buy a dictionary, thesaurus, atlas, or almanac in the book corner of the shop. Martin and Son was no office supply store, but a haven for those who relish the heavy solidity of a really good pen or the lush pigment of a well formulated ink or the feel of quality paper.

The first thing Olive noticed on coming down the back stairs and into the shop was, however, not the merchandise, but a ginger tabby cat who had made itself quite at home outside the front windows, where there was a long flower box just under the bottom of the pane. In the spring, it would be brimming with zinnias, alyssum, and petunias in every color, but in February, it was full of snow. And apparently, one well-fed cat.

"Hi, Gwen," Olive said, startling the young woman who had been concentrating on the book that lay on the counter in front of her.

Gwen's face lit up when she saw Olive. She shut her book—a tattered copy of William Shakespeare's *Hamlet*—and jumped off her stool, ran around the counter, and enveloped Olive in a huge hug. "I'm so glad you're home!"

Olive who at thirty-two, used to babysit the seventeen-year-old, hugged her right back. "Me, too."

"How's the bookbinding business?"

"Good. Just finished repairing a six-volume set of old Will's works, as a matter of fact," said Olive, nodding toward the copy of *Hamlet* that still lay on the counter. "Leather bound first editions, if you can believe that. They were sent to me by a rare book seller in Oregon. So, how's life in St. Drogo?"

"Good," Gwen said with a nod. "I have a literature test tomorrow. That's why I'm studying." Gwen had been working at Martin and Son since she'd started high school, and gladly spent her after-school hours, as well as some of each Saturday, there. "How's Henry?"

Olive sighed. "They said he's asleep right now, but I'm about to head over to the hospital anyway. Are you here for the whole afternoon?"

"Right up to closing," said Gwen with a nod. She put a hand on Olive's shoulder. "I'm sure he'll pull through. He's in great shape. And poor Malcolm, well, he had other health issues that made his case more complicated."

Of course, Olive knew all of this. She'd been saying the same things to herself for days. But for the first time since Malcolm Warbly's death and her father's illness, Olive felt like she might cry. She nodded at Gwen and swallowed the lump in her throat. The two went on to catch up on what was happening at the shop and in town, and how Gwen's family had been doing. Gwen beamed when she told Olive about her new boyfriend, and how he was taking her to Friday night's Valentine's dance.

"By the way, who's that?" Olive pointed to the cat in the window, who had apparently finished his grooming and was now intently watching them.

"Oh, that's Oscar. At least that's what I call him, because I was reading *The Picture of Dorian Gray* by Oscar Wilde for school the first time I saw him. He's a stationery lover for sure because he always sits there in the window looking in."

"Who's his owner?" asked Olive.

"I don't think he has one," said Gwen.

"Well, someone's clearly feeding him."

"The coffee group gives him scraps. And so do the restaurants up and down Cornwall Row."

Olive walked over to the window and tapped it. The cat raised hazel green eyes to her and blinked, almost as if smiling his own *Welcome home.* "Hello, Oscar."

The bells above the door jingled and a customer came in—a tall, well-dressed man with brown hair and matching mustache.

"Hello, Mr. Northam," Gwen said quickly. "Still thinking about that limited edition St. Germaine Classique with hand-crafted 18 karat gold nib embellished with the etching of the Eiffel Tower?"

"How'd you guess?" the man said with a smirk. Then he walked to the back corner, where Gwen, hurrying along behind him, unlocked the glass case and brought out the pen. At almost a thousand dollars, such a pen was an investment, to be sure, and Martin and Son had always allowed customers to test out their pens and take their time deciding.

Gwen left Mr. Northam in the corner with the pen and the scratch pad of one hundred GSM paper they always kept out for testing anything from luxury pens to ballpoints.

"That's Pavel Northam—from Northam Estate?" Gwen whispered to Olive.

"Northam Estate? Where's that?"

"You know—up on Amber Hill?"

Olive thought for a moment. "You mean the old Harcourt mansion?"

"Yep. Mr. Northam bought it about two years ago and has been painstakingly renovating it ever since. And he renamed it, of course."

"Isn't that place haunted?"

Gwen snickered. "Apparently the ghosts of the Harcourt family don't like having their home redone. There have been all kinds of mishaps at the build from what I hear. Just little things, like missing lumber and knocked-over cans of paint. But frustrating nonetheless." She looked back at Mr. Northam. "Isn't he dashing?" she whispered.

Olive looked back. "I guess. In a sort of James-Bond kind of way."

A Fine Point of Murder

As they were sizing him up, Mr. Northam gingerly set down the pen and moved over to the book corner, flipping through the dictionary that Olive's dad always kept on the antique lectern.

"Still working on expanding your vocabulary?" Gwen called with a laugh.

"Absolutely," said Mr. Northam with a wink over his shoulder. "I try to learn a new word every day."

Just then, the bells above the door jingled again, and in came Andy Spelling—an old friend of Henry's and one of the members of the shop's unofficial coffee-drinking group.

"Well, here she is!" Andy said, setting his newspaper and book on the counter and opening his arms wide when he saw Olive, who ran over and hugged him. "How's your papa doing today?"

"Sleeping right now. I'm about to go check on him."

"He's tougher than nails, you know. He'll pull through." He shook his head. "Terrible, about Malcolm though."

"Yes," said Olive. She glanced down at the half-worked crossword puzzle and dictionary on the counter. "Still keeping sharp with those puzzles, I see."

Andy pointed at his head. "Got to keep the juices flowing," he said with a chuckle.

"So, how's the security business been treating you?"

"Can't complain," said Andy. "Just got a promotion, in fact. Head of security at Pottsleigh."

"Wow! That's amazing!" Pottsleigh Manor was the town's other great estate, ranking just above the newly-named Northam House in stature, and it was still owned and inhabited by the Pottsleigh family. It was a historical landmark *and* a mark of pride for the whole community and had stood on a hill to the west of town since the time of Queen Victoria. In fact, St. Ann's Creek, which wound its way around the manor, along past town, and then veered around Amber Hill —joined it to the possibly haunted Northam House. It was said that the two estates had once been at odds, the two families embroiled in a battle for status and power in the area back in the day. But, the Pottsleighs had remained and the Harcourts had died out or moved away.

A Fine Point of Murder

"So have you talked to the doctors over at the hospital today?" Andy asked.

But before Olive could answer, the door swung open again, and Chester MacDonald bustled in. He also had a big bear hug for Olive. "We thought you'd be home today. Good to see you, girly." Chester himself was a big bear of a man, always clad in a hat—which in the winter was his Irish tweed flat cap. He owned a clock and watch shop, Tempus Fugit, just around the corner on Cornwall Row, which was St. Drogo's busiest street.

Right behind Chester were the final two members of the coffee group, Miles Handicott and Maeve Pickering. Miles was head librarian and director at St. Drogo Public, and Maeve, a retired elementary school teacher, owned a children's book and toy shop, Scattergoods, which was just a few doors down from Chester's clock shop.

Everyone was thrilled to see that Olive was home. They buzzed about her for a few minutes, asking how long she could stay and how Henry was faring and wondering what they could do to help.

Finally, they were ready to head out the back door into the courtyard that stood between the back of

Martin and Son and their favorite coffee shop, St. Drogo's Cup. It was their routine to meet around this time, late in the morning but before lunch. They'd lumber into the stationery shop, collect Henry and Malcolm, and then trickle out the back door to order coffee and sit and chat for an hour or more, then go on about their days. When Gwen came over on her lunch break from school, she stayed inside and watched the shop. But much of the time, Henry and Malcolm just went out to the courtyard and propped open the back door, keeping an ear open for the bells above the front door inside. Thankfully, there was little to no crime in St. Drogo, so no harm ever came of the coffee hour.

Just as they were turning to head outside, Maeve elbowed Andy. "Why not invite Mr. Northam to join us for coffee?" she whispered, peeking over at the stylish Northam, who was still flipping through the dictionary.

"Nah," said Andy. "He's too high society for the likes of us."

Maeve blew out a *pffft* sound. "You're just jealous because he's so—"

"So *what*?" asked Andy, raising a brow at her.

A Fine Point of Murder

"Debonair," said Maeve.

Andy opened the back door and bowed with a flourish. "My lady," he said, inviting Maeve to go out first.

"We'll see you later, darlin'," said Chester as he followed them out.

"Let us know how your dad's doing after you go to the hospital," added Miles, going out last.

Shortly after that, Mr. Northam also left the shop, saying he'd be back soon, and Gwen settled herself behind the counter with her book.

"I'll just check Dad's date book in his office and then head over to the hospital," said Olive, giving Gwen a wave.

She opened the weathered oak door and went into the little room. Henry's office was the larger of the two offices at the back of the shop—Malcolm's being the smaller. Henry's even had a window that looked out into the courtyard. Olive looked out now, and smiled to see the coffee group, sitting at their usual table, not minding the cold one bit as they bent over steaming cups of coffee and talked with great animation.

Olive turned to her father's desk, where, as usual, the datebook lay open to the current week. She checked over this week's entries, making sure there were no important appointments that needed to be addressed. "Oops. He won't be getting to Dr. Albert's for his six-month checkup," Olive mumbled, opening the drawer and digging for a pen. She'd have to call the dentist and reschedule.

Henry's pen tray was buried underneath a bunch of papers in the top drawer—which was uncharacteristic, since Henry always kept a tidy desk, both inside and out. Olive took out the stack of pages and found a pen, dialed Dr. Albert's office, and wrote the new appointment in for two weeks later. She felt a pang of worry. Would her dad be well by then, and up to getting his teeth cleaned?

As she was putting the papers back into the desk, she took a better look at them.

"What's this, Dad?" she mumbled, frowning at the pages. They appeared to be rubbings, made with the edge of a pencil lead, revealing the markings—mostly gibberish—that had been made on another sheet of paper. Olive scanned page after page, unable to make sense of any of them, save the one where Malcolm had written his own name in fancy script. Dear old Malcolm. How was it possible that he was gone, that Olive would never see him again?

She'd have to ask her dad what these papers were doing in his desk. Instead of returning them to the drawer, she stuffed them into her bag and hurried upstairs to run a brush through her hair before heading over to the hospital.

CHAPTER 3

Henry Martin was just waking up when his daughter peeked into his room.

"Well, there you are," he said, his face lighting up at the sight of her.

Olive hurried to his bedside. "How are you feeling, Dad?" She brushed a hand through his hair—which was still thick and mostly dark, but with flecks of gray running through it.

"Never better," Henry said, then flinched a little.

"You're in pain."

"Well, now. Maybe a little." He flinched again.

"I'm calling the doctor—"

"Now, now." Henry reached out and touched Olive's arm, stilling her. "Just let me talk to my daughter for a few minutes. Then we'll call the doctor. Okay?"

Olive nodded, willing any stray tears not to fall. She pulled a chair up to Henry's bedside and sat. "How are you feeling, *really*?"

"There's a certain amount of pain," Henry admitted, patting his stomach. "I think I'll pull through." His smile faded into deep sadness.

"I'm so sorry about Malcolm."

Henry nodded. "Me, too." He sniffed. "Good man. Good friend." He squeezed his eyes shut for a moment, then seemed to shake it off and looked at Olive. "So, how's things down at the shop? I assume you checked when you got to town?"

"I did," said Olive. "The coffee group had just arrived when I left."

"Those nutters," said Henry with a laugh. "They'll help keep an eye on things until I can get back to work."

A Fine Point of Murder

"Oh, Dad—I was in your office and found these odd papers," said Olive, opening her bag and pulling out the stack of rubbings. "What are these?"

Henry squinted at the papers, then reached over and grabbed his reading glasses from the tray table beside him. "Oh those. I have no idea what they are, to tell you the truth. I was supposed to bring them to Malcolm here in the hospital. He told me to get them from his desk. But then he—" Henry took his glasses off and set them back on the table. "Anyway, I don't know what they are." He grimaced and clutched his stomach.

Olive stuffed the papers back into her bag. "I'm calling the doctor." She hurried out into the hall and caught a passing orderly. "My dad needs help. Immediately."

The orderly nodded and jogged off. Olive returned to Henry's side, and within a minute, the doctor rushed in. Olive stood back as he checked her father's vitals and palpated his stomach a bit. He brushed past her and stuck his head out into the hallway. "Nurse!" Then he came back into Henry's room and produced a tiny penlight from his pocket and shone it into Henry's eyes. "Where is that nurse?" he grumbled, glancing over his shoulder, his eyes catching on Olive.

"Olive!" he said.

Olive did a double take. "Peter? Peter Tremblay?"

Peter Tremblay had been *that guy*, back in school. Handsome. Smart. Athletic. Every girl had a crush on him—and Olive was no exception. Olive had lost track of him through the years—had lost track of most of her graduating class, for that matter. And now he was a doctor.

Another man—who wasn't quite as tall as Peter, his dark hair and beard a little shaggy in contrast to Peter's perfectly styled hair and clean shaven face—rushed into the room. He wore medical scrubs and had a stethoscope draped around his neck. "Could you move back a bit please?" He gave Olive a stern look.

Olive's eyes caught a glimpse of his name tag. *Nurse Noah Whitby*. This was the nurse! Olive inwardly scolded herself for having assumed the nurse would be female.

"Sorry," she mumbled.

"Let's boost his pain meds a bit," said Peter, taking out a pen and pad, scribbling instructions and handing the page to Nurse Noah Whitby. "And please monitor his vitals."

The nurse looked at him, frowning as if insulted. "Of course, doctor." He said it politely, but Olive saw his jaw clench and release a few times.

Peter turned to Olive. "Olive, this is Noah Whitby. He's head of nursing here at St. Drogo Medical Center. He'll be overseeing your dad's case."

Noah barely glanced at Olive.

"Nice to meet you," she said.

He gave her a quick nod and a little grunt but was clearly focused on his work—which Olive considered to be a good thing. He tapped a syringe and jabbed it into the port on Henry's IV.

"So, Olive," said Peter, pulling her aside a bit. "How have you been?"

"Good," said Olive. "What do you make of Dad's condition?"

"It's very strange, but we're working on figuring it out. I've put a rush on the autopsy of Mr. Warbly since he presented similar symptoms. It's possible they caught the same virus or ingested the same food… It's just too soon to say for sure. But I will say, I believe your dad is faring better than Mr. Warbly did."

"Thank heaven for that," said Olive, looking over at her dad, who appeared to have nodded off. "He's as tough as a boot."

"Does that run in the family?" asked Peter with a grin.

"I hope so," said Olive, managing a smile.

"How about dinner tonight? I'd love to catch up."

"Well, I—" Olive looked back over at her dad.

"You have to eat and sleep if you want to help your father," said Peter.

He was right, of course. "I'd love to. Where should I meet you?"

"How about Top of the Row?"

If Olive wasn't mistaken, Noah emitted another little grunt—but it probably wasn't directed at them. "Top of the Row. Fancy," she said. The restaurant, well known and revered all over the area, sat on a charming corner of Cornwall Row and River Road, surrounded by large trees with lanterns that hung from their branches. Olive had eaten there before, of course—but only three times in her life, all of them very special occasions.

"They make a great seafood chowder, with fish and bacon and potatoes, and the chocolate potato cake is heaven on a plate."

"That does sound wonderful," said Olive, who had always had a weakness for chocolate potato cake—a rich dessert that was loved all over the island.

"Meet you there at seven," said Peter. He patted her arm. "We're going to take care of your dad. We're going to figure this thing out and get him well," he assured her. "He needs to rest a bit. The pain medicine makes him sleep."

Olive nodded. "I'll check back later."

She started to leave, glancing back at her dad one last time. Noah was just carefully tucking a blanket in around Henry, and the grumpy scowl had been replaced by a gentle smile. Olive heard him speaking softly. "It's going to be okay, Mr. Martin. Don't you worry."

Olive let out a breath. She hoped Noah was right.

CHAPTER 4

When Olive walked through the front door at Martin and Son, Gwen was just coming inside from the courtyard out back. The shop was quiet, with no customers at the moment—which was not unusual for a small town stationery store on a Thursday afternoon.

"How's Henry?" Gwen asked.

"I'm not sure, to be honest," said Olive, feeling herself shuddering a little. "Dr. Tremblay says he's doing better than Malcolm was, although it does seem to be the same sickness. And you know my dad." Olive grinned. "Tough as nails."

Gwen walked over to Olive. "I'm sure he'll beat this."

"Thanks, Gwen."

Gwen gave a little nod, then walked back around to her perch at the counter and looked down at her book. "So . . . Dr. Tremblay, huh?"

Olive could see the small smile playing at Gwen's lips. "We're having dinner tonight."

Gwen looked up. "Seriously? You *just* got into town, and you already have a date with the local hottie?" She caught herself. "I mean, all the ladies within a fifty kilometer radius, of pretty much every age and persuasion, have crushes on him."

"Well, I don't," Olive said, walking toward Malcolm's little office. She paused and turned back, grinning. "Although I might have, back in the day. We went to school together. Peter's an old friend."

"Old friends make the best boyfriends," Gwen sang.

"*Please.*" Olive rolled her eyes and opened the door to Malcolm's office. She stopped dead in her tracks when she saw the room. It had been ransacked. Every drawer and cabinet stood open, books had been pulled off the bookshelves, some of the inventory Malcolm kept on hand was strewn about, and files and papers were spread all over the desktop. The first thought Olive had was how much Malcolm would *hate* this. The man—from his pressed handkerchiefs to his collection of Italian leather shoes which were never scuffed—was always neat as a pin. His office was the picture of full-blown organization. "Gwen? Could you come here please?"

Gwen gasped on seeing the office. "I hope Malcolm can't see this from the great beyond. What happened here?"

"Someone was clearly looking for something—and in a hurry to find whatever it was," said Olive. When Gwen started to take a step forward, Olive grabbed her arm. "We'd better stay outside the office until the police can come take a look. I wonder how long ago this happened."

Gwen looked at her watch. "Had to be within the last fifteen minutes."

"What? Seriously?"

Gwen nodded. "I came in here to get that sample ink Malcolm had sent off for—the Riverton in the olive green? I remembered he'd wanted at least one of the good pens loaded with it for customers to try. That was just after you left for the hospital. Everything was in perfect order then."

"And you've been here all day since then."

"Yep. Well, except for when I went outside with the coffee group. But I was out there for maybe five minutes. They were debating where to get the best oysters in town, and I was their tiebreaker. Andy and Chester were for Tad's Pub, but Maeve and Miles said Macadoo's." Gwen cleared her throat, looking abashed. "Sorry about that."

"I hope you went with Macadoo's," said Olive, trying to help Gwen feel better. "Well, then, at least that leaves a very small window of time that the person could've come in and done this." Olive grabbed the phone and called the police. When she hung up, she took a deep breath to steady her nerves. "They'll be here shortly." Her cell phone rang, and she pulled it out of her pocket.

"Olive? Peter Tremblay."

"Oh. Hi, Peter." Olive glanced at Gwen who, in spite of the dire situation in Malcolm's office, managed a smile.

After a short conversation, Olive clicked off the call and put her hands on the counter, taking a few more deep breaths, feeling far from steady now.

"Olive? What is it? Is Henry okay?"

Olive suddenly felt a little breathless and was starting to get lightheaded. "No—I don't know. I hope so."

"Sit down," Gwen ordered, taking Olive by the arm and leading her around to the other side of the counter, then guiding her into a chair.

After a moment, Olive felt the blood returning to her head and managed to slow her breathing. "Peter just saw the results of Malcolm's autopsy," she whispered, looking at Gwen. "He was poisoned." She swallowed. "Malcolm was murdered."

CHAPTER 5

Olive stopped for a moment and stood looking at Top of the Row from the cobbled sidewalk out front. Glimmering lanterns hung in the branches of the many large trees that surrounded the building, casting a warm glow over the whole scene. Smaller trees strung with twinkling lights lined the front walk, gently arching over it, so that just making one's way to the front door was a magical experience in itself. The exterior of the restaurant was of an old, aged brick, and large windows offered dimmed glimpses of the people inside, sitting at tables that were scattered with flickering candles.

If the place itself was impressive, the food served there was even better. Top of the Row was famous for its cuisine, which was an ironic and delectable mix of gourmet and home cooking. There was nothing haughty about the items on the menu, and yet they'd taken old favorites to new and unexpected heights. Even from outside, Olive could smell the chocolate potato cake—a special recipe that Beatrice, the head baker, prided herself on. The moist, rich confection needed no frosting—it was that good.

Olive inhaled deeply, closing her eyes for a moment.

"Makes you want to skip right to dessert, huh?" Peter had walked up behind her and lightly placed a hand on her back.

Olive turned to him, smiling. "You read my mind."

They went inside and since Peter had made reservations, they were shown at once to a quiet corner table with windows overlooking the beautiful yard outside, with a "Right this way, Dr. Tremblay," from the host. Within seconds, they had menus in their hands, iced water in their glasses, and napkins in their laps, and were left to decide what to order.

As they perused their menus, Peter asked Olive about her afternoon, and she told him about what had happened at Martin and Son.

A Fine Point of Murder

"How horrible. What did the police say?"

"Well . . ." Olive hesitated.

The local chief himself had come straight over to the scene, along with another officer. Olive's heart had sunk a little when she'd seen that the chief was Clark Walters—not because Clark wasn't highly qualified or anything like that. It was just that he was in his twenties—early twenties to be exact—and Olive remembered how, when she was about twelve, she'd helped babysit him in the nursery at Rolling Hills United Church. Mrs. Valentine, who acted as the church secretary and also oversaw the nursery, had always appreciated Olive coming in on Sundays when extra little ones showed up for the service. Olive would play with the older kids—one of whom was the future police chief. But Clark was only four years old back then. Looking at him in his uniform today, Olive kept having flashbacks of him playing with the police and firefighter uniforms from the costume trunk.

"Mrs. Valentine? The church lady?" Peter snickered after Olive told the tale. "She's still there, you know. Father Stan may be the rector, but everyone knows Mrs. Valentine runs the place. I get what you mean, though—about Clark. It's hard to have full faith in the crime-solving abilities of a person you used to play Chutes and Ladders with."

"Candy Land," said Olive, shaking her head. "Clark always wanted to play Candy Land. How did he get to be chief of police so young?"

Peter laughed. "Did you see his trusty deputy, Sam Stalks? He looks about fourteen."

"Maybe they're not that young," said Olive. "Maybe we're just getting old."

"Not a chance," said Peter, giving her a wink. "It's just that there's basically no crime in St. Drogo. For that matter, the crime rate is pretty low all over the island. But here, other than the occasional parking violation or pie stolen out of Mrs. Lark's kitchen window, there's just not a lot for a police officer to handle. The seasoned professionals probably prefer to work elsewhere—just to avoid boredom if nothing else."

"Mrs. Lark's pies," said Olive with a smile. "I'd forgotten about those."

"Her blueberry is second to none."

"I'd consider stealing one of those. Anyway, Clark and Sam came and looked at the mess in Malcolm's office, declared that someone had definitely been there searching for something, attempted to check the room for fingerprints, and then proceeded to spill the fingerprint powder all over the place. So, we have an even bigger mess to clean up and no leads as of yet."

"And the police only told you what you'd no doubt already surmised yourself," added Peter.

Olive looked at him. "So, Malcolm had been poisoned?"

Peter nodded solemnly. "Deadly Firecap."

"The mushroom? Seriously?"

"Yep. That explains why it didn't kill him for a few days. It acts a lot like the famous Deathcap mushroom. Doesn't kill you until it attacks your liver. Poor Malcolm."

"Is there any chance he wasn't murdered—that he accidentally ate the mushroom?"

Peter shook his head. "Not likely. You know what the Firecap looks like, with that bright orange top. Everyone around here knows."

"So, it was in something he ate, you think?"

"Or drank. It wouldn't take much to kill a person. And Malcolm wasn't in great shape to begin with." He looked earnestly at Olive. "Your father, on the other hand, is fit as a fiddle. And now that we know what got Malcolm, we know how to treat Henry. They're running the tests as we speak to confirm the diagnosis."

"So, there's an antidote?"

Peter sighed. "I wish there was. But there is an appropriate treatment protocol. He has every chance of beating this." He reached over and touched Olive's hand. "We didn't know what was wrong with Malcolm, so we didn't know how to treat him."

Olive nodded, feeling a little breath of relief. "Thank you, Peter. I feel better just knowing you're watching him."

"Not to mention Nurse Noah. He's like a mother hen. He and your dad have been getting along famously. He's been voluntarily putting in extra hours just to keep an eye on Henry."

Olive was surprised, thinking of the grumpy Noah. But then she pushed aside her memory of the way he'd talked to *her* and remembered the way he'd talked to her father, with such kindness and care. She felt a sense of peace, knowing that Noah was by Henry's side.

After a delicious and fortifying dinner of hearty chowder and salads followed by thick slices of chocolate potato cake and coffee, Peter walked Olive home. It was a chilly night, but the stars were out in full force, and when they arrived at the side staircase that led up to the apartment, Olive stopped and turned to Peter.

"Thanks for dinner. It was wonderful." She suddenly felt bone tired and wanted nothing more than a hot bath and a comfortable bed.

"Thanks for going," said Peter, taking one step closer to her and tilting his head slightly to the right as though he might lean in and kiss her. But then he didn't. Instead, he said, "I know these aren't ideal circumstances for a first date, but I hope we can try again tomorrow night. There's the annual Valentine's dance at the Feed Store and I'm hoping—if and only if your dad is doing well—that you'd like to join me. Everyone will be there."

The Feed Store hadn't been an actual feed store for decades, although it had been one in the past and the name had stuck. These days, it was a favorite local party place—charming, with its old stone walls, huge fireplace, worn wood floors, and wide open space. It could be dressed up or down and was the perfect spot for any shindig or reception or celebration. The people of St. Drogo descended on the place for a dance on the Friday nearest Valentine's every year.

Olive wasn't at all sure she'd be up to going under the circumstances, but on the other hand, if Henry was getting better now that they'd be treating him properly, the dance would be a lot of fun, not to mention a great opportunity to see friends she hadn't been in touch with for a while. She agreed to go with Peter, and he smiled and gave her a hug.

Olive headed upstairs, and within ten minutes, was climbing into a tub filled with hot water and bubbles. As she leaned back and felt her muscles loosening up, she replayed that hug in her mind. Peter Tremblay—*the* Peter Tremblay—had made close physical contact with her and had invited her to the Valentine's dance. Why didn't she feel at least a little flutter in her stomach or a little lift in her heart? The hug had felt more like an embrace from a good friend. Olive sank a little deeper into the bubbles. It was probably just because it had been such a long day—a million years since she'd crossed the bridge to come onto the island. She closed her eyes and relaxed. She would get a sound sleep and tomorrow would be a whole new day.

Suddenly, she heard a sound. A clatter followed by a muffled thud. Then another thud. She sat up and listened. There it was again. Was someone downstairs in the shop? Olive quickly hauled herself out of the tub and wrapped herself in a thick robe. She listened again. Nothing. She rushed around silently, looking for a weapon of some kind and ended up grabbing an umbrella from the stand next to the door. She crept a few steps down the inside staircase, listening all the while, hearing nothing, and then taking a few more steps. At the bottom of the staircase, she slowly opened the door to the shop and peered in. There, sitting in the middle of the main room floor, licking his paws, was Oscar, the ginger tabby cat she'd seen outside earlier. She hurried over and scooped him up. "What are you doing in here?"

Oscar blinked serenely and nuzzled Olive's cheek with his velvety nose.

She scratched him behind the ears. "If you think you can get into my good graces after scaring me like that —" Olive froze, having glanced at her father's office door.

It stood ajar, even though she was certain she'd locked it at closing time. She crept a little closer, and saw that the door's window had been broken, and the room itself had been ransacked in exactly the same fashion as Malcolm's office.

Olive ran up the stairs, taking Oscar with her, and locked and bolted the apartment door behind them. She called 9-1-1, and the emergency dispatcher assured her the police were on the way. Olive looked at the little cat. "Thank goodness they didn't hurt you —whoever they were." Oscar looked up at her, purring loudly. Olive caressed his soft, striped fur. "You know, we're in the market for an official stationery shop cat. Up for it?"

CHAPTER 6

Young Chief Walter's approach to investigating the second ransacked office was much the same as the first. It seemed the tiny St. Drogo police department wasn't exactly equipped or trained for advanced CSI. Clark did surmise that the culprit had been wearing gloves, so no fingerprint evidence could be collected. It was as clear as day that someone was desperately searching for something at the stationery shop, but it was anyone's guess as to what that might be since nothing appeared to be missing and nothing was stolen. Clark and Officer Stalks took Olive's statement and said they'd file a report and be in touch.

The next morning, Olive awoke with a start. Something was tapping her on the forehead. It turned out to be a padded little paw.

"I take it you're hungry," Olive said, looking into the unblinking hazel eyes of Oscar, who was perched on the next pillow over, which he'd claimed as his own the night before. A quick stop in her bathroom revealed that Oscar had made use of the bathtub as well. "Let's make a quick run to the pet shop and get you a litter box," said Olive. "And some food."

Luckily, the local pet shop, Whiskers, was just a short distance down and across Forest Lane. Olive bought everything Oscar could possibly need or want, hoping her dad would be okay with having a cat around. If he wasn't she would simply take Oscar with her when she left to go home.

Home. Where was that, even? She'd always thought of St. Drogo as her home, like some traveler who tromps around the world but always returns to the same place eventually. She just hadn't settled down yet. There would be time to think about all those things later, though. For now, the management of Martin and Son and getting her dad well were enough to occupy her mind. And since she was between bookbinding jobs, there was no clock ticking.

She stopped in at St. Drogo's Cup for coffee before heading back to the shop, where she got Oscar fed and settled, then showered and dressed in simple slacks, boots, and t-shirt with a favorite cardigan sweater. It didn't take long to blow dry her chin-length dark hair, add a few swipes of mascara and lipstick, and trot down the inside stairway, Oscar following at her heels.

The morning was spent tidying up her father's office in between helping customers. Gwen would be arriving at noon, so Olive stayed busy. The coffee group trickled in late morning, all of them shocked by the news of what had happened the night before.

"Where's Andy?" Olive asked, realizing he was the only member of the group who was missing.

Maeve sighed. "Seems there was a string of crimes here in town last night."

"I think *a string* implies more than two," said Miles.

"What happened?" asked Olive, petting Oscar, who'd just jumped up onto the counter.

"The estate where Andy works—Pottsleigh Manor?" Maeve started.

"It was robbed!" said Chester.

"Andy's down at the police station now. He arrived at work this morning to find the safe open and some very valuable jewels missing." Maeve shook her head. "Apparently it happened last night while Andy was down at the theater with Chester."

"We saw that new spy movie," Chester put in.

"So, Andy didn't do his usual walk-through last night," Maeve continued. "He left one of the underling guards in charge. Anyway, Andy is just devastated. He feels like it happened on his watch so it's his fault."

"So, the house is guarded overnight?" asked Olive.

"Round the clock," said Maeve. "The family comes and goes a lot, which is why they hired Andy to oversee security. Andy said the junior guard didn't even know the robbery had taken place until early this morning if you can believe that. Apparently the thief knew exactly where the jewels were kept, cracked the safe, *and* the alarm failed. Well,"—she blew out a breath— "you can imagine how Andy feels right about now."

"He's a mess," said Chester, nodding.

"But let's talk about something positive," said Maeve, a smile growing on her face. "I hear there was a very handsome couple dining at Top of the Row last night."

Olive felt her cheeks going pink. "Peter's an old friend."

"A very dashing old friend," said Maeve.

"That's what we need," said Chester with a chuckle. "You fall in love with a good St. Drogo boy and stay here—where you belong."

Olive found the thought strangely comforting. After all, it is a wonderful thing to belong somewhere.

"So do the police have any idea what your intruder could be looking for here?" asked Miles.

"No. Nothing appears to be missing," said Olive. "I can't help but wonder . . . You're going to think I'm crazy, but . . ." She took out her bag and pulled out the stack of papers she'd found in her father's desk.

She hadn't shown them to Clark because frankly, she'd been in shock at the time—and besides, she couldn't imagine the young chief would have known what to make of them. But somewhere in the back of her mind, she'd wondered what they were. And now, she wondered if perhaps—however unlikely—it was possible that the intruder had been after them. After all, they had been in Malcolm's possession first, and he'd given them to her father. Maybe the intruder knew that, and so logically had looked in Malcolm's office first, then moved on to Henry's. "What do you make of these rubbings?" She spread the papers out on the counter. "I found them in Dad's office shortly after I got into town. They'd been given to him by Malcolm, but Malcolm died before explaining them to Dad."

"They look like pages from the tester paper," said Maeve, glancing over to the corner where customers could try out pens and pencils.

"And someone—Malcolm, I'd guess—has made rubbings of the pages that were on top of these . . . you know, like you did when you were a kid playing spy games. He's revealed what someone had written on the pad." Miles flipped through the pages. "Mostly just scribbles and—" He paused, and his eyebrows came together. He straightened his wire-rimmed glasses and took a closer look. "Hold the phone. This might be a code."

"What? Really?" Olive, along with Maeve and Chester, leaned in closer.

"We need coffee and lots of it," said Miles. "Let's go out to the courtyard and try to crack this."

The group trailed out the back door into the sunny winter day.

"Let me know what you find out!" Olive called after them.

The bells over the front door jingled and Gwen came in just as the phone rang. Gwen grabbed it, then handed it right to Olive. "It's the hospital," she said, her face clouding over with concern.

"Hello?"

"Hi, Olive. It's Peter. You need to come over here. Now."

CHAPTER 7

Olive rounded the corner and caught sight of her dad—and was pleasantly surprised. Henry Martin was sitting up in bed, the color had returned to his cheeks, and he was eating a bowl of soup.

"Got any extra? I'm starving," Olive said, dragging a chair over to the bedside.

"Nurse! Bring this woman a sandwich!" Henry called, the old twinkle back in his eye.

Noah poked his head into the room. "Do I look like a waiter? Next thing I know, you'll have me going out for pizza."

"Pizza sounds good," said Olive, giving him a smile.

He frowned at her. "Can I see you outside for just a moment?"

"Of course." Olive's heart picked up a bit. Maybe there was bad news after all, and the nurse didn't want her dad to hear. She gave Henry a kiss on the cheek and stepped into the hallway with Noah.

"I just wanted to apologize," he said, glancing at his feet, then at his clipboard, then at his watch. Finally, his eyes moved back to her face. "I was rude yesterday—I didn't mean to be."

"Oh." Olive breathed a huge sigh of relief. "I thought you were going to say there was something else wrong with Dad."

"Oh. Sorry."

"No! That's okay. I'm glad. I mean—" Olive noticed that Noah's eyes were the same hazel color as Oscar's. He really was quite handsome in a sort of rugged, outdoorsy way—when he wasn't scowling. Olive cleared her throat. "Thanks. For taking such good care of Dad. I—uh. Thanks." Could she have flubbed that any worse?

"Oh, Henry's a pleasure to work with," said Noah. He led Olive back into the room and shifted his attention fully over to his patient. "Good job on the soup," he said, inspecting the empty bowl.

"I'd rather have a hamburger," said Henry, winking at his daughter.

"Clear liquids and bland food for now," said Noah.

"You see what I have to put up with?"

Just then Peter swept into the room. "How's my favorite patient doing today?" He spotted Olive. "How'd you like your surprise?"

"Wonderful!" said Olive.

"Bet you'll be in the mood for the Valentine's dance tonight," he said with a chuckle.

"I know *I* am," said Henry. "Maeve and I can cut a rug—"

"Not you, Mr. Bojangles," said Noah. "Not until you're stronger."

Olive's cell phone rang. It was Gwen, calling to check on Henry. Apparently the whole coffee group was gathered around the phone, because Olive could hear them cheering when she told them the good news, that Henry had turned the corner and would soon be on his feet again.

"Hey, Henry, we're coming over later!" Olive heard Chester yell. Then there was another round of applause, and Olive got off the phone.

"Sounds like you'll have some company soon," she said to Henry.

"Just what the doctor ordered," said Peter with a laugh.

"That and a fun evening for you, out with your friends," Henry added, patting his daughter's shoulder. When Olive started to protest, he shook his head. "I'm going to be fine, darling. You go out tonight and have enough fun for the both of us. Okay?"

CHAPTER 8

Almost all of St. Drogo turned out for the annual Valentine's dance that evening. The Feed Store had never looked lovelier. Twinkling red and gold lights were strung from the rafters, clusters of pink, cream, and rose gold balloons graced the stair railings and support columns and arched over doorways. A fire crackled in the stone fireplace, and soft music wafted through the air. Every head in the place turned when Dr. Peter Tremblay walked in with Olive Martin on his arm. Olive noticed that most of the older women smiled, looking pleased as punch. Many of the much younger women seemed to take on admiring glances and whispered among themselves. Those in their late-twenties to mid-thirties smiled, but with a hint of resentment behind their eyes which Olive might or might not have imagined. And the general male population gave friendly glances—well, other than one of them. Noah Whitby was standing across the room, and when Olive caught his eyes, he looked like he'd returned to his old grumpy demeanor.

With all the attention, Olive was suddenly self-conscious in the extreme, and wondered if Peter often elicited this reaction from a crowd. She looked at him, his confident smile unmoved, looking textbook handsome in his khaki pants, chambray shirt, tweed blazer. He was, she realized at that moment, possibly *the* most eligible bachelor in town—a son of St. Drogo, one of a long line of Tremblays who had lived in the area. Well-respected, well-bred, well-educated, and well-off to boot.

"Everyone's looking at you," Olive mumbled through the smile she'd pasted on.

"Nah," he said, sidling up to the punch bowl and ladling out a cup. "It's you they're looking at. You're by far the most beautiful woman here."

Olive immediately felt her cheeks getting warm. "I think a few of the other ladies are hoping I won't keep you all to myself."

Peter handed her a glass of punch. "Too bad for them," he said with a laugh. "Now. Drink your punch. Then I'm going to sweep you off your feet and onto the dance floor."

A few minutes later, they were dancing. Peter's movements were practiced and smooth—an easy partner. He spun Olive around, then pulled her close with perfect finesse.

"You're actually managing to make it look like I know how to dance fairly well," said Olive, exhilarated by the way he'd just effortlessly dipped her.

"Well," he said, lowering his voice, "some people just naturally make good partners."

Before she could blush again, Olive changed the subject. "How was Dad when you left the hospital?"

"Getting along famously. He's definitely on the mend. In fact, his whole coffee group was just arriving as I was walking out of the building, and I even gave them permission to have a cup with him. They'd brought a couple thermoses full from their favorite coffeeshop."

"St. Drogo's Cup," said Olive, nodding. "By now, they're probably playing a rousing game of dominoes or gin, cutting up like they always do."

"Best medicine there is," said Peter.

The song ended and Olive spotted Gwen, who was standing at the desserts table with her boyfriend.

"How about a little dessert? I'd like to go say hello to Gwen," said Olive.

They moved through the crowd, stopping here and there to chat with friends. Olive got more hugs and *welcome home*s than she could count. By the time they reached the dessert table, she felt well and truly happy. Maybe she'd stay in town a while, even after Henry got out of the hospital. After all, she could do her work from anywhere, and there wasn't another place on earth where the people knew her name and knew her family, where she was rooted in deep like she was in St. Drogo. Just the smell of the air alone—a singular mix of the distant sea, the grasses and trees and flowers that grew in the area—felt like home. And Olive hadn't felt that for a while now. She'd forgotten the gift of *belonging* in a place, like Chester had said.

Gwen introduced Olive and Peter to her boyfriend Justin Plum. Justin was extremely polite and a little shy and frequently pushed his glasses up his nose. After only a short conversation, Olive heartily approved of him for Gwen.

Suddenly Peter's beeper sounded. He took it off his belt and read the words. "It's the hospital." He looked apologetically at Olive. "I'm going to have to step out for a few minutes. Don't worry. It's not your dad. It's about another patient of mine."

"Of course," said Olive, nodding. "Take all the time you need."

Olive continued sampling desserts and chatting with Gwen and Justin for the next few minutes. She was startled when a hand touched her shoulder and she turned to see Noah.

"Hi—sorry, I didn't mean to scare you. I was wondering if you'd like to dance."

Olive glanced toward the door through which Peter had exited and caught sight of him pacing along the wide front porch, still very engrossed in his phone call. "Okay," she said, taking the hand Noah held out.

He started to lead her to the dance floor, but Gwen stepped forward.

"One second, Olive. I almost forgot." She set down her plate and opened her bag. "Miles left a note for you at the shop when he was on his way over to the hospital tonight. He asked me to deliver it to you since I told him I knew I'd be seeing you here tonight. He said it was important and that he'd follow up with you later." She handed Olive a folded slip of paper.

"Thanks," Olive said, taking the note and tucking it into her pocket. She took Noah's hand again and he pulled her into his arms. The song was slow, and there was no twirling or dipping, but Olive had the disconcerting sense that there was something between her and Noah. She felt something. Something she hadn't felt when Peter had hugged her goodnight after their dinner out, or even when she'd danced with him. Noah was so different. But as the two of them swayed to the music, Olive felt her body relax into his. He smelled good. Now and then, she saw that Peter was still outside, on the phone.

"So, what's the note about? Do you know?" Noah said into her ear.

Olive snapped out of her temporary daze. "I think it's

probably about this code Miles was trying to crack earlier." She explained to Noah about the rubbings she'd found at the shop, and about how Miles, ever the librarian, had taken them to do a little digging and try to decipher them—if, indeed, there was anything to decipher. "Miles was convinced they were a secret code," she explained.

"That's fascinating," said Noah as the song ended and he released her. "Let's see what the note says."

Olive unfolded the page and read. "This is amazing. Miles says he actually did crack the code!"

They moved over to the dessert table, rejoining Gwen and Justin, who had moved on from the cake to the cookies. Peter came over as well, apologizing for the long phone call. Olive brought everyone up to speed about what Miles had been up to and finished reading the note, her eyes widening further with each line.

"I can't believe this. It's about a robbery! The code was about a robbery, Miles thinks. He says it's what's called an Ottendorf cipher."

"What's that?" asked Gwen.

"Oh! I know this!" said Justin. "It's a book cipher. The code uses a book that both the sender and receiver have access to. Usually, it's done in a series of three numbers. The first number is the page number, the second is the line number, and the third is the word number. You look up a group of these number series and write down each word. The words go together to form the message."

"In this case, Miles figured out which book was being used because the first note included the call numbers," said Olive.

"And Miles is a librarian," said Gwen, nodding.

"Miles says that if he's right, the sender has supplied the receiver with the location and combination of a safe, as well as the time the robbery should take place . . . and he says the book used in the cipher is the First College Dictionary."

"That's the one we have at the shop!" said Gwen.

"Yep," said Olive.

"This has to be the robbery that just happened at Pottsleigh!" said Noah. "I heard about it on the radio on the way over here."

"Pottsleigh Manor was robbed?" asked Peter.

"Yes," said Olive. "Just last night. Andy from the coffee group is head of security there, and he was—"

"Wait a second!" said Gwen. "Mr. Northam! He's always testing the pens on that pad—the pad where that paper came from! And he flips through the dictionary—"

"To improve his vocabulary!" Olive finished. "That's right!"

"Wait. Are we talking about Pavel Northam? From Northam House?" asked Peter. "I've met him." He frowned in confusion. "Are you saying he wrote those notes?"

"No," said Olive, coming to a sudden jarring realization. "I think he *received* them." She felt her stomach turn over as she realized something else. "I think Andy wrote them."

"Andy—" Gwen paled. "Andy Spelling? From the coffee group? No, surely not."

"Think about it. Andy's in the shop almost every day. He buys all his pens there and tries them out routinely. He carries a dictionary for his crossword puzzles—the same one we have on display in the shop."

"Are you sure about that?" asked Noah. "For the code to work, it would have to be the same edition and everything."

"I'm sure because we sold him that dictionary. It's the only one we carry," said Olive. "I remember because I was in town at the time, and Andy had spilled coffee on his old dictionary, so Dad gave him the new one at cost. We all laughed about how Andy was coming out ahead on the deal. And Andy is head of security at Pottsleigh."

"So, you think Andy gave Northam information about how and when to crack the safe," said Noah, crossing his arms over his chest.

"Right," said Olive. "And he made sure it happened when he wasn't there, so he wouldn't be the obvious culprit. He left an inexperienced guard in charge. Let's face it, if anyone knew when and how to rob the place, it'd be him. But he couldn't do it alone."

"Makes sense," said Noah.

"This is awful," said Gwen.

"I'm calling Clark—I mean, Chief Walters—right now," said Olive, taking out her phone.

Peter's beeper went off again and he read the message. "Oh no. This time it *is* your dad. I told them to alert me if there was even one peep from his room."

"The coffee group is at the hospital! Andy is there!" said Olive, feeling her heart pounding in her throat. "We have to get over there immediately. Peter! Call the hospital and make sure Dad doesn't drink the coffee. Tell them you'll explain when we get there. I don't want Andy to overhear and make a run for it."

"I'll drive," said Noah. "You call the police. Let's go."

CHAPTER 9

Everyone had piled into Noah's old jeep, with Peter frantically calling the hospital, Olive frantically calling the police, and Gwen and Justin squished into the back, just holding on for dear life. Noah got them from the Feed Store, which was on the outskirts of town, to the hospital in record time. They all went running in, Peter and Noah leading the pack, skipping the elevators in favor of the stairs. When they reached the second floor, they flew down the hall and burst into Henry's room.

There sat Henry, propped up in bed, looking as well as he had before. Maeve and Chester stood next to him, one on either side. There were concerned looks on all three faces.

"Dad? You're okay?" Olive had to bend over with her hands on the bed to catch her breath.

Henry opened his arms and Olive made her way to the head of the bed and hugged him. "I'm fine, darling. It's Miles."

"Miles?" Olive looked around. No sign of Miles. "Where is he?"

"They're admitting him."

Noah and Peter rushed out of the room.

"Stomach pump?" Olive heard Noah say as they disappeared around the doorframe.

"Miles drank the coffee. You didn't. Right?"

Henry looked at his daughter. "How did you know that?"

"Where's Andy?"

Henry looked around. "He was here a minute ago." Then he snapped his fingers. "I bet he's gone to call the Pottsleighs," he said. "There's a police scanner down at the nurses' station. We just heard they arrested that Mr. Northam that always comes into the shop. Can you believe it? He was the thief who robbed Pottsleigh Manor!" When Olive didn't respond, he put a hand on hers. "What's going on here?"

Olive looked at the two thermoses sitting on the bedside table with five cups around them. "I figure one of those thermoses is full of coffee that's been poisoned."

Maeve and Chester both gasped at once.

"And I'd be willing to bet that you two drank from the same thermos as Andy did."

Maeve nodded. "Henry and Miles prefer dark roast. Andy insisted they have their favorite, what with Henry on the mend and Miles cracking that code."

"Did Miles tell you what the code meant?" Olive asked.

"No," said Maeve, a little frown coming to her face. "He didn't want to talk about it at all, in fact. He said he wasn't positive yet."

"Didn't want to talk about it in front of Andy is more like it." Olive looked at Gwen. "Better call the police. Andy's making a run for it."

Gwen and Justin left the room to make the call.

"Andy . . . And Mr. Northam . . . And Pottsleigh." A light dawned in Henry's eyes, then he looked at Maeve and Chester, who seemed to have just arrived at the same conclusion.

"Oh my," said Maeve. She looked at Chester. "Let's see if he's still in the building. The police can't get here quick enough."

Chester nodded and the two hurried out of the room. Henry tried to get up and follow, but Olive pushed him back into the bed. "The police will handle it," she assured him. "It's not safe and you're not that strong yet. Let's just wait here together, okay?"

Henry sighed and nodded, then leaned back on his pillows. Olive picked up the nearest thermos and took the lid off, giving it a tentative sniff. "Thank heaven you didn't take a drink."

"They told me the doctor had called and said I shouldn't," said Henry. He shook his head slowly. "Here's to following the doc's instructions."

"Too bad I'll have to kill you anyway."

A Fine Point of Murder

Olive and Henry both turned to see that the bathroom door had opened—and who should be standing there, pointing a gun at them, but Andy. His usually sweet, round, pink face was contorted with an ugly glare, and beads of sweat were forming on his upper lip.

"Andy! What were you doing in there?" Henry asked, his voice wavering just a tad.

"I thought these bathrooms had windows, but yours doesn't. Looks like I'm stuck. And that means the only way I'm getting out of here is with a hostage. So, which of you will it be?" He looked back and forth between Olive and Henry as though trying to decide, then landing on Olive. He took a step toward her.

"Take me," Henry said quickly.

Andy's eyes shifted over to Henry.

And it was at that very moment that the spirit of the venerable St. Drogo must have filled Olive with divine inspiration. In one swift movement, she threw the hot coffee in Andy's face. He dropped his gun, which fired off a shot at the wall as it struck the ground. A loud hubbub could be heard in the hallway in response, and within a few moments, several nurses, Chester and Maeve, and Chief Walters came rushing in.

"Poison!" Andy yelled, jumping around in a panic. "Some of the coffee got into my mouth and eyes. I need medical treatment!" When no one rushed to help him, he wailed, "It was the dark roast!"

CHAPTER 10

Oscar hopped up onto the counter and rubbed up against Henry's arm.

"I go to the hospital for a few days and come home to find I have a cat." He shook his head.

"About time you let this sweet little gentleman into the shop," said Maeve, reaching out to give Oscar a scratch under the chin. He purred loudly in response. "He's been loitering outside for months. That's true devotion."

"Plus, he'll guard the place," added Chester with a chuckle. "Just look at those claws."

The bells above the door jingled and Miles came in, looking a little tired, but mostly recovered from his own short stint in the hospital. Everyone gave a little cheer, Gwen and Olive included, and Miles took a bow.

"About time you got here," teased Henry. "Now we can go out back and have our coffee."

"I think I'm switching to tea," Miles joked.

"Sacrilege!" shouted Chester.

"Blasphemy!" added Maeve. "This is St. Drogo!"

Henry looked at his three friends. "I guess we'll have to recruit another member or two for the coffee group, now that good old Malcolm is gone."

"And Andy is in jail," added Maeve. "That scoundrel."

"Greed," pronounced Chester. "Corrupted by greed." He shook his head sadly. "You think you know a guy . . ."

"So, this all started over at the Nip-In?" asked Henry.

"Yup," said Chester. "Our young Chief Walters got the full story between Andy and Northam. Apparently Andy was there, celebrating and shooting his mouth off after he landed head of security at Pottsleigh, and how he'd be guarding those fabled jewels."

"And how Mrs. Pottsleigh was taking the dupes on their trip to Europe," said Maeve.

"Dupes?" said Olive.

"Yep. She has a whole set of exact duplicates of her most valuable jewelry—never even takes the real ones out of the safe apparently," said Maeve. "Seems like a waste to me."

"I agree," said Henry, grinning at Maeve. "You'd never want anything gaudy like that."

Maeve returned the grin and gave a little half-shrug. "Nothing wrong with a nice gemstone here and there."

"But I don't understand," said Gwen. "Mr. Northam has his own estate. He's loaded. Why would he want to risk everything to rob Pottsleigh Manor?"

"Because Northam House is a money pit," said Henry. "The place is falling apart. I remember thinking Northam was in over his head back when I heard he'd bought it."

"So, he needed the money . . ." said Gwen, nodding.

"Enough about all of this," said Maeve, turning her smile to Olive. "I hear you have a date tonight."

Olive felt her cheeks burning. "I do."

"A nice St. Drogo boy is just what you need," said Chester.

Olive laughed. "I hardly think a man in his thirties could be called a boy."

"Then he's a lucky man," said Chester.

A large truck pulled up in front of the shop, its brakes squealing as it came to a stop. Henry nodded to his friends. "You three go on out to the courtyard and order. You know what I like. I'll be out momentarily."

Maeve, Chester, and Miles headed out into the courtyard, Gwen went off to clear out Malcolm's old office, and Henry turned to his daughter. "So, we have a cat now. And Malcolm's old office is going to be yours. What else do you have in mind for the shop?"

A Fine Point of Murder 73

"A new website. A strong online marketplace. A few decorative updates." Olive smiled at him and then added, "A bookbinding service."

"Oh." A crease formed between Henry's eyebrows as he looked out at the truck, who's driver was just hopping out and walking up to the door. "There's one more change. I hope you don't mind. I made a command decision without consulting you, partner."

"You did? What was it?"

"Come with me." They walked out the front door, and Henry greeted the truck driver and his helper. "Let's see how it turned out," he said, giving the man a wave.

"Sure thing," said the man, signaling his helper. "Go ahead."

The helper pulled a canvas cover off the huge item that was tied down with cables in the truck bed.

Olive stepped closer to have a look.

"It's a new sign for the shop," said Henry, a note of pride in his voice.

"*Martin and Daughter*," Olive read. "*Stationer. Bookbinder.*" She looked at her father, tears filling her eyes.

He wrapped her up in a warm hug. "I'm glad you've finally come home, my girl."

She looked at her dad. "Me, too. Thank you, Dad."

He scoffed. "I've got to get out to the courtyard. Don't want to keep the others waiting too long." He glanced up the sidewalk. "Oh—and it looks like your date has arrived."

Olive turned to see Noah, who was walking toward them, looking a little nervous, carrying a small bouquet of pink roses in his hand.

Henry elbowed her. "Sure would be nice to have a nurse in the family," he said, earning him a swat from Olive. Henry gave her a quick peck on the cheek. "You two have fun this evening. Oscar and I will hold down the fort." He sighed, looking contented. "I'm just so glad you finally found your way back."

Olive smiled at Henry. "It's good to be home."

. . .

Top of the Row Chocolate Potato Cake

Ingredients:

-1 cup cold mashed potatoes

-2 sticks (1 cup) unsalted butter, softened

-2 large eggs

-2 cups brown sugar (You can also use granulated sugar, or a cup of each!)

-1 teaspoon vanilla extract

-1 teaspoon almond extract

-2 cups flour

-1/2 cup cocoa powder

-1 teaspoon baking powder

-optional: confectioners' sugar for topping

Instructions:

Preheat the oven to 350 degrees. Cream the butter and sugar in a large mixing bowl until nice and fluffy.

Add the eggs and beat until fully incorporated. Add the mashed potatoes and the extracts and mix.

In another bowl, mix together the flour, cocoa powder, and baking powder. Then add half the dry ingredients into the butter mixture plus half the milk. Mix that up and then add the other half of the dry ingredients and finally, the last of the milk. Mix.

Spray a 9-inch springform pan with cooking spray. Pour the batter in and bake for around 45 minutes—maybe a little longer. A toothpick inserted into the center should come out clean. After the cake has cooled for around ten minutes, run a knife around the edges of the pan and remove the ring. Then let the cake cool the rest of the way. Sprinkle with powdered sugar and enjoy!

Note: If you want to make a layer cake, grease and flour two 9-inch cake pans and bake at 350 degrees for 25 minutes or so. Maybe 30. Test with the toothpick. Once cool, frost with your favorite frosting. We like cream cheese or caramel frosting with this cake!

AUTHOR'S NOTE

I'd love to hear your thoughts on my books, the storylines, and anything else that you'd like to comment on—reader feedback is very important to me. My contact information, along with some other helpful links, is listed on the next page. If you'd like to be on my list of "folks to contact" with updates, release and sales notifications, etc.… just shoot me an email and let me know. Thanks for reading!

Also…

… if you're looking for more great reads, Summer Prescott Books publishes several popular series by outstanding Cozy Mystery authors.

CONTACT SUMMER PRESCOTT BOOKS PUBLISHING

Twitter: @summerprescott1

Bookbub: https://www.bookbub.com/authors/summer-prescott

Blog and Book Catalog: http://summerprescottbooks.com

Email: summer.prescott.cozies@gmail.com

YouTube: https://www.youtube.com/channel/UCngKNUkDdWuQ5k7-Vkfrp6A

And…be sure to check out the Summer Prescott Cozy Mysteries fan page and Summer Prescott Books Publishing Page on Facebook – let's be friends!

To download a free book, and sign up for our fun and exciting newsletter, which will give you opportunities to win prizes and swag, enter contests, and be the first to know about New Releases, click here: http://summerprescottbooks.com